Green Goo

There is green goo on my plate that I know I will hate. But mom says I should not say 'hate', that it's not the right thing to do. It is hard to think what else to say as I stare at my plate in dismay.

The green goo shivers and quivers as I tap my fork on the side of my plate. While I sit and stare, it is as if the pile of green goo grows. Soon the green goo will touch my nose.

This is my fate, this pile
of green goo on my plate.
Mom says if I ate it I
would be done and then I
could go play and have fun.

Maybe I could slide the
green goo onto my lap, but
it will soak through my
pants. It's so slimy and wet that
it will attract ants.

Maybe I could drop
it on the floor.
When no one else is
looking I could shove
it out the door.

But then the green goo might
get stuck on my shoe. I
might slip and slide. Maybe I would
hit my head. I could end
up dead. That would never do.

Maybe I could feed it
to my dog. He will
eat anything. But what if
it turned his fur green?
That would be mean.

My sister seems to like it.
She smiles while she dips a
chip in her green goo. She
slurps it up noisily and doesn't
take the time to chew!

But what is the green goo?
Is it a fruit or a vegetable?
If I eat the green goo,
how do I know it won't make
my tongue scream, "Ooo, ooo, ooo?"

I want to take a bite but it fills
me with fright. If I put it on
my tongue I am afraid it will sit
like a big blob. It will ooze
and grow, becoming a giant glob.

It could close off my throat and make me choke. Or it could be worse. What if it crawls back out when I try to swallow and it makes everyone laugh till they howl?

Dad says the green goo is from an avocado. They call it guacamole after they mash it into this paste. It doesn't sound so bad now that I know its name. I might even dare to take a taste.

av·o·ca·do
/ˌavəˈkädō,ˌävəˈkädō/

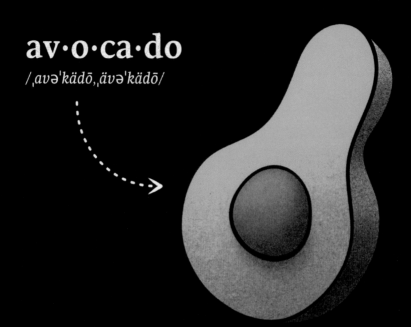

gua·ca·mo·le
/ˌgwäkəˈmōlē/

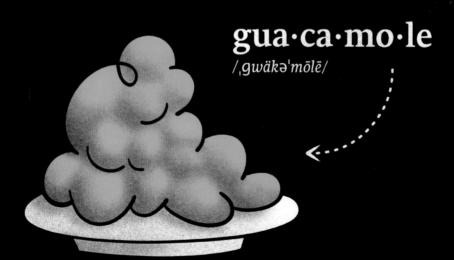

I know I like the way
the chips taste and crunch.
Dad says it is just a
hunch, but he thinks I
will like green goo a bunch!

I really do want to try it. I
don't want my sister to think I am
a little kid. Maybe I should have a
barf bag just in case. I sure hope
the goo doesn't dribble down my face.

Here I go! I'll take a
little dip with a big chip.
I won't let it touch my
lip. Just crunch and chew real
fast. Hey, that was really good!

I guess the green goo on
my plate is something I don't hate!

THE END

Made in the USA
Monee, IL
09 December 2020